# THE STORY OF SECRET HEART

## A BEST LOVE STORY NEVER SEEN BEFORE

AKASH MAHAPATRA

Made with ♥ on the Notion Press Platform
www.notionpress.com

## The Story of Secret Heart

The face is the mirror of the mind, and eyes without speaking confess the secrets of the heart.

-Jerome

# Contents

*Contents* *vii*

1. The Beginning Of The End 1

2. The Turning Point 5

3. The Tug Of War 6

4. Overcoming Obstacles 7

5. The Road To Redemption 8

6. A New Beginning 9

7. The Reunion 10

8. The Struggle To Succeed 11

9. First Bike 12

# Contents

Introduction: The Story of Secret Heart

- Story
- First Bike
- The beginning
- Love
- Heartache
- Freedom
- A Strager in my Life
- New Beginning
- Dating
- Feelings
- Different Universe
- Work
- Ancient History
- Travel
- Family
- First Time
- Bad Time
- Sister
- Canberra
- Another Place
- A Companion
- The Bettle Begins
- Move On
- Doing stupid things
- Favour
- Party
- Confidence
- Fun
- Money n More
- Coco

CONTENTS


- New Home
- Dinner
- Airport
- First time for everything
- My Choice
- Decissio

# 1

# The Beginning of the End

In a small town I live. When I was seventeen, at the time of becoming an adult. I feel that I head in love with a girl; also I went to College with her. She wasn't the most popular girl in College or the most most smartest girl, or the most talented, or the most athletic, or even the wealthiest. But simply I'm going to say that she is the most sweet, cute and kind hearted & the funniest girl of my class. She used to make me laugh & my whole body would ache and after that also I'd have to beg her to stop.

Ofcourse at that age, what about my parents else every parents didn't agree with anything I did, and hanging around with that, is no exception. I was a good student and Mathematics is one of my Favourite Subject. So, I thoroughly read, practise it and also I score a good rank in it. For, the first time Paa (my father) drop me off at her house. That time he (Paa) is very averse/ disinclined/ hesitant to let e even go to a young girl's home/ house, but that time I was seventeen and there wasn't much he could do about it.

As we drove, Paa eyed the area with vigilance and asked me,

"*What the hell do you see in this boy?*"

And then very honestly I answered,

"*She is very good girl and also she makes makes me laugh.*"

Paa responded spontaneously with, "Yes, well."

> "*A woman's heart is a deep ocean of secrets.*
> *- Gloria Stuart*"

> "*Secrets of the Heart are seldom news.*
> *- Jennifer Stone*"

**One year Later,**

One year later, after the distance with each other, I thought this was the end of this stuffs. But as time passed, I realized that my feelings for her were still there, buried deep within me. I couldn't stop thinking about her and all the memories we had shared together. I knew that I had to see her again, to find out if there was still something between us. So, I gathered up my courage and decided to visit her at her home. I remember the drive there, my heart beating fast with anticipation and a touch of fear. Would she be happy to see me? Would she still feel the same way about me? I had no answers to these questions, but I knew that I had to try. When I arrived at her house, she greeted me with a warm smile and invited me in. We sat down and talked for hours, catching up on old times and reminiscing about the past. And as we talked, I realized that my feelings for her were still as strong as ever. I knew that I had to tell her how I felt, to take the chance and see if she felt the same way. So, I took a deep breath and confessed my love for her. And to my surprise and delight, she told me that she felt the same way. We talked about our future together and decided that we wanted to be together, no matter what anyone else thought. With that, we started our new journey together, facing the challenges and obstacles that came our way with love and determination. And as we looked back on that day, we knew that it was all worth it, because we were meant to be together.

As we started our new journey together, we knew that there would be obstacles to overcome. Our families were not entirely on board with our relationship, and we faced a lot of resistance and disapproval. But we were determined to make it work and to prove to everyone that we were meant to be together.

We spent every moment we could together, building a life and a future. We went to college together, and I continued to excel in my studies, especially in mathematics. She was my rock, my support, and my inspiration. She helped me to see the world in a new light and to believe in myself. As we graduated from college, we faced new challenges. We had to find jobs and a place to live, and we had to navigate the complexities of adult life. But through it all, we stuck together and supported each other. We knew that as long as we had each other, we could accomplish anything. And so, we moved forward, building a life and a future together. We faced our challenges head-on and emerged stronger and more in love than ever before. And as we looked back on the years that had passed, we knew that we were truly blessed to have found each other and to have built a life together.

Despite their deep love for each other, the SAM's lover (PRIYA) is forced to marry another guy by her family and relatives. She is torn between her feelings for the main character and her duty to her family. The main character is devastated and struggles to come to terms with the news. SAM tries to move on and focus on his own life, but he can't help but think about his lover (PRIYA) and what could have been. He is filled with regret and a longing to be with her. Meanwhile, his lover is also struggling with her feelings and her new life. She is unhappy in her marriage and longs to be with SAM.

DRAMA & CONFLICT:

As SAM and his lover struggle with their feelings, the husband of PRIYA (ROHIT) finds out about their past relationship. He becomes furious and confronts SAM, threatening him to stay away from his wife. To make things worse, SAM's father, who had disapproved of his relationship with the lover in the past, also finds out about the ongoing situation. He is furious with SAM and forbids him from seeing the lover again. Feeling trapped and torn between his love for the lover and his duty to his family, SAM is forced to make a difficult decision. He decides to stay away from the lover, despite the heartache it causes him.

But as fate would have it, the lover's marriage falls apart and she is left alone. SAM and his lover are once again reunited and this time they decide to be together at any cost. They decide to leave the small town and start a new life together. But their happiness is short-lived as ROHIT comes to know about their plans and decides to take legal action against them. Now SAM and his lover are in a legal battle, and the story takes a dramatic turn as they fight for their love and freedom.

After a horrible distance with each other I thought this was the end of this stuffs. And then moved on, and that was the end of that. After that things, which i felt and then decided that, my dad was right.

# 2

# The Turning Point

# 3

# The Tug of War

# 4

# Overcoming Obstacles

# 5

# The Road to Redemption

# 6

# A New Beginning

# 7

# The Reunion

# 8

# The Struggle to Succeed

# 9

# First Bike

I got my first bike in the time of winter on Durga Puja Sale of 2020, when I was just eighteen years old. After seeing so many guys ride their bikes, I figured it was my turn to shine at this. I felt such an adult boy, all grown up, my Paa took me to the Showroom to choose one. I sat on a chair untill I finally liked one. It was navy Blue with a mixture of white and dark and even it come with matching wheels and with dual Channel ABS, which was perfect. I was feeling very good to show off my to all of my colleagues and students, I went to college with.

After i got home, I loved my brand new bike to the point where i even felt like bringing it into my room to sleep next to. The next day came, however, I was too frightened to ride it because this is my first nd new bike if it damaged/ cracked. How on the earth would I be able to control that enormous chunk of metal? I thought. It remained in my home for the next month simply since I refused to ride it, In reality, I was too scared.

I did know that I was an easy quitter, but I really did not care; to be honest, it was kind of a pathetic. Once, my Paa came home, from his office and he basically took my bike out and dragged me to the park against my wanted terms. He sat on the back seat, as he told me to get on the bike. I began to ride and I started to wobble but he didn't even let me fall once. I became confident that he would be there even if I did fall. On the other hand, he was confident that I would succeed this time. He knew the exact right time to let me go, and when to loosen his grip. I've been able to see his support and this love time after time. He wasn't afraid to let me wobble just a bit and he knew to never make the mistake of holding on with a firm grip that would prevent me to learning how to navigate through on my life.

ᢇᢇᢇ

Printed by Libri Plureos GmbH in Hamburg,
Germany